LIFEBOAT

America Reborn

John Dale

The politics of left and right won't matter when we all go broke.

GEORGE ERIKSON

CONTENTS

PROLOGUE

You probably have opinions about George Erikson, and about his legacy. But how much do you really know about this private but influential man? What was he thinking, and worrying about, during the critical phases of our recent history?

The man whose ideas gave birth to a new Republic was not easy to find, and even harder to get a meeting with. "I'm just not that interesting," he said during my second phone call requesting an interview. "A rancher north of here has a white buffalo calf. You should go talk to him." I knew what I was up against; and frankly, I sympathized. After more than ten years of an increasingly public life—a life he never wanted—he had successfully faded into the background over the last half-dozen years. Even if he had been interested in talking about himself, and he most certainly was not, he wasn't likely to accept the risk of more public exposure.

Taking advantage of his innate politeness, I called a third time and he agreed to discuss my idea for this book. However, it soon became clear that he was not going to allow me to write a traditional biography. "First of all, the story shouldn't be about *me*. The story should be about what *we* as *Americans* got done, and are still getting done. Second, biographies are boring, even when they're about interesting people." For a brief moment, I thought I was going to get Iron George to bend; but in the end, there it was. Take it or leave it. I had exerted complete editorial control over the six books in the *Jack Moss Biographies* series, but if I wanted a meeting, I —a professional and experienced biographer—was going to be strong-armed by his subject into writing a history. Ultimately, he allowed me to include details about his life and his motivations, and those are woven into these pages.

I took a cab from my apartment in New York to the airport, where I caught the first of the two flights it would take to get to Jackson, Wyoming. The next morning, when I headed south from Jackson in my compact rental car for our meeting at his house, I didn't realize how long I would be driving. After what seemed like an eternity, I arrived at the unmarked entrance to his property and headed down the long dirt driveway, despite there being no building in sight. I was about to turn around, when I saw a surprisingly small farmhouse.

He smiled when he saw me stretching after I got out of the car. "Distances out West are longer than you'd expect, aren't they?" he said. "Imagine you, the great Jack Moss, coming all the way from the USA just to see me." He waved me inside, but in a sly glance back at me he noticed that I was looking at the house. "You were expecting something bigger,

8

weren't you?"

He was right, and when I stammered, trying to think of a nice way to say that the house didn't quite match the property, he chuckled and said "That's what happens when your political conscience undermines your own pension."

As we were about to enter the house, he stopped, turned directly to face me, and took a deep breath. "The bad news, Mr. Moss, is that my wife is out, so you'll have to suffer through my coffee and cooking. I'm a decent cook for breakfast, but you just missed that. The good news is that I feel like talking today, and I'm going to tell you everything I can. It's quite a story. I hope they let you write it."

Jack Moss
August, 2046

CHAPTER 1

Warning Signs

> *The idea that there were two Americas—red and blue—missed the point. There were supposed to be fifty.*

GEORGE ERIKSON

INTERVIEW

JUNE, 2046

"Well, 2020 was an awful year, even though it didn't turn out to be the disaster that many thought it would be. I remember being disappointed by people's willingness to just throw debt at the COVID-19 problem, and by the hysterics that substituted for a discussion about race, but every problem of that year was what we in the military called a 'survivable wound,' and we survived them. That being said, the cracks already in the foundation got a little wider that year." He recalled 2020 as being the first time, at age 39, that he became concerned about how Americans looked increasingly to the federal government for solutions instead of considering the local or state level. "This trend of 'federal first' had been going on for years," he said. "But that's when it really sunk in for me."

George Erikson and I had been talking about the separation movement for about an hour, but the movement had only begun in 2033, and I wanted to ask about earlier influences. After his comments about 2020, I asked him to reach back further and talk about his upbringing. "Well, I was born not far from here on July 3rd, 1981..." then he paused, and burst out laughing. "You should see the look on your face! I *told* you it was not going to be that kind of book!" I admitted he surprised me a little bit, and we laughed, but I took the opportunity to ask about his parents. "Well, I should talk a little about them, because the way they raised me had a lot to do with how I think."

Erikson's mother was from rural Mississippi. After meeting his father in a history class at the University of Wyoming, they eventually married and settled down in their college town of Laramie. She became a tenured professor of political science, and he was a history teacher and football coach at a local high school. The dinner-table debates were epic.

"I spent years trying to figure out which of my parents was liberal, and which was conservative," Erikson began. "Sometimes, it seemed like they took different sides of an argument just so they could needle each other. What I finally figured out was that they would often oppose each other to show me how to form a logical argument, and how to disagree with *civility*. When I look back on it, the way they spoke to each other was remarkable. They batted facts back & forth like it was a tennis match; sometimes lobbing them over the net, sometimes firing the ball down the line. But it was always about *facts*, not *feelings*. The goal was always to discuss policy, what worked, or what might work; not personal passions or aspirations."

There were two things that the elder Eriksons always agreed upon. The first was the importance of individual liberty. Each embraced a classical liberal view expressed by George's father with the phrase "maximum freedom of the individual without infringing upon the rights of others," a summary of the philosophy of John Stuart Mill. A second issue they agreed upon was the corrosive impact of long-term debt. They weren't concerned about the kind of debt families would have. Like most families, the Eriksons had a mortgage on their house, but it was a modest house that was within their means, and the mortgage was paid off around the time George left home for college. They were concerned about the *national* debt, and the U.S. Government's increasing tendency to pay for today's programs with tomorrow's money. "It would be like me packing your lunch for school, and then eating half of it," his mother would say. "Sure, the government uses terms like 'quantitative easing' and 'intergovernmental holdings' to shield what it's doing, but the fact is unavoidable: our government is borrowing—stealing—money that will not be available to future generations." The last time George could remember his mother talking about debt, right after he graduated high school in 1999, our national debt stood at just under $6 trillion, or about *two-thirds* of our Gross Domestic Product (GDP).

In 2010, about the time George had finished graduate school after leaving the military, the Chairman of the Joint Chiefs of Staff, Admiral Mike Mullen, said "the most significant threat to our national security is our debt." Most retiring generals at the time, when asked about looming threats, would say something about Chinese military growth, Russian cyber-hacking, or the Iranian nuclear program. Nobody in his position had ever said anything about debt, and it summarized what Erikson came to believe whole-heartedly, and what would guide his actions over the next several decades: our greatest enemy was *our own spending*, and the policies that spending forced us to adopt.

At the time of Admiral Mullen's statement, the U.S. Government's debt was about $12 trillion, representing by then three-quarters of GDP, and the annual interest payments on that debt were nearly as large as the defense budget. (Were it not for the wars in both Iraq and Afghanistan, the interest payments would have been larger than the defense budget.) "I thought that was bad," said Erikson, "but a mere ten years later, in 2020, the federal debt had *doubled again* to over $24 trillion! It had taken the United States over 230 years to reach $12 trillion in debt, and we doubled *that* in a decade." Worse, the U.S. government debt was now larger than GDP for the first time since World War II. And of course, the debt problem didn't stop there.

When one considers the values upheld by Erikson's parents—liberty, civility, and frugality—it becomes clear why 2020 was such a disappointing year for George, and for the country. With respect to liberty, people proved all too willing to give up "essential liberty for temporary security"—thereby getting (and deserving) neither, just as Benjamin Franklin warned us about. While the

COVID-19 pandemic was a serious issue, it did not require the suspension of both the legislative and judicial processes that accompanied that crisis. It would have been far better, and far more legal, for issues like mask mandates and business closures to have been passed by legislation instead of executive orders. Civility, for its part, went out the window following the Black Lives Matter protests and riots that summer. "The nation completely stopped talking about policy, and the national debate got caught up in 'identity politics.' According to the loudest voices of the day, innate factors—such as what color you were, or your sexual preference— were somehow supposed to drive your views about public policy. It was beyond nonsense. It was offensive."

Worse still, the focus of debate was mostly about what the *federal* government should be doing about both issues—the disease and the police, whose actions were the focus of the rioters' anger. "Sure, it was an election year, and anything, even a disease, will be political in an election year; but as I said before, this habit of looking to Washington had been on the rise for a while." Overlooked in both cases, as in many issues, was the fact that no national policy could be appropriate, or efficient. "In 2020, Manhattan—just one borough of New York City— had nearly three times as many people as the whole state of Wyoming. Why should our public health policies be the same? Why should our police act the same?

"Indeed, as Supreme Court Justice Louis Brandeis famously said: 'a single courageous State may, if its citizens choose, serve as a laboratory; and try novel social and economic experiments without risk to the rest of the country.' We were never supposed to be a singular nation. We were supposed to be a Republic made up of united but individual states."

While the Erikson family values of civility and liberty both suffered in 2020, by far the most lasting casualty of that summer was frugality. Shamelessly trumpeting the politician's maxim of "never let a good crisis go to waste," politicians saw opportunities, especially in the COVID-19 crisis, to fund and grow their favorite programs. The money that was wasted on non-disease issues within the various, enormous "COVID-19 relief" bills has been well-covered in other books and articles. "Everyone gasped when the debt surpassed GDP that year," George recalls "and then just as quickly forgot about it. But the debt didn't forget about us."

CHAPTER 2

From Debt to Dependency

> *Freedom is ... not an endlessly expanding list of rights — the "right" to education, the "right" to health care, the "right" to food and housing. That's not freedom, that's dependency. Those aren't rights, those are the rations of slavery — hay and a barn for human cattle.*

P. J. O'ROURKE

"I've only read two books that scared the crap out of me," George said, out of the blue. We had talked the morning away, and now it was time for lunch. In truth, *Erikson* had talked the morning away, and I had scribbled furiously in my notepad despite his allowing me to use a tape recorder. "You're lucky," he said after looking in the fridge. "We have some leftover lasagna, so you don't have to endure my cooking after all." I would have paired the lasagna with red wine instead of lemonade, but I was thirsty, starving, and wine wasn't on the menu. Midway through a relatively quiet lunch, it was clear that he now wanted to talk about books.

"The first book doesn't have a title, because it was actually a brochure." After serving for five years as an Air Force officer—a job that took him to Alabama, Hawaii, and Kuwait—young Captain Erikson left the military to join the Department of Defense as a civilian. "I took a job in procurement at the Pentagon, and thought it would be my job to help the military buy the best planes, ships and weapons for our armed forces. After all, I had just spent five years learning everything I could about them while I was in the service." He chuckled. "I couldn't have been more wrong if I'd tried." No longer Captain Erikson, *Mr.* Erikson would soon learn that while the military had *some* input to the procurement process, it was actually members of Congress who called the shots.

"All the big defense contractors made large,

glossy brochures about their products that were es-
sentially tailored catalogues for congressmen. The
typical format involved a full-page glossy photo of
the defense system in question—rifle, tank, computer, whatever. The facing page would have bullet
points about the system in question, and a color-
coded map of congressional districts that high-
lighted where each component of the system was
manufactured."

He laughed again, apparently at himself, and then
continued. "Picture a naïve, young Mr. Erikson
being called into a meeting with a Congressman,
having been invited to what he thought would be
a substantive discussion about the merits of a particular air defense system. When I arrived, the
Congressman asked 'did you bring the books?', in-
dicating one of the brochures I described. When I
said yes, he took it joyfully and said 'Thanks! These
things are real time-savers!' He then proceeded to
flip through the book, spending about one second
per page and only looking at the congressional district maps. 'No...No...No...Yes...No' he intoned as
an aide took notes. It was one of the most discour-
aging episodes of my professional career. My advice
and experience meant nothing. The needs of the
soldiers, airmen, sailors and marines meant nothing. The only criteria that mattered in the whole
process, at least as far as this representative was
concerned, was the political impact on his district.

"The second book that scared me came out a

few years later. It was written by a man named Peter Schweizer and titled *Extortion: How Politicians Extract Your Money, Buy Votes, and Line Their Own Pockets.* Although I was already becoming cynical by the time it was published, this book convinced me that the situation was actually worse than I thought."

For those not familiar with the book, it describes how the traditional view of corruption in Washington D.C.—that businesses and special interests reach out to politicians in order to corrupt the legislative process—was actually outdated and inaccurate. What was happening, in fact, was that Congressmen shook down businesses routinely; threatening to enact damaging legislation unless businesses and/or their employees made donations to political campaigns or action committees. Worse still, in the all-rules-are-made-to-be-broken (or re-written) climate of Washington D.C., the money would not only be used for campaigns, but would actually fund the lavish lifestyles of elected officials and their families. "This was personally revolting to me as a public servant," George added, "and I also began to wonder if the system was fixable. Could new rules prevent this sort of corruption, or were Congressmen too entrenched and untouchable to reform themselves?

"I took a shot at fixing this in 2031, but everyone knows how that turned out. It was pure folly, and maybe even vanity, to think I could have fixed anything. Many had tried, and all had either been corrupted by the system they sought to reform, or resigned in disgust. I should have known better." Although I had been focused on the earlier years of George's life at this point in the interview, he skipped ahead to refer briefly to his single term as a U.S. Senator from Wyoming.

"Besides," he continued, "*discretionary* spending —the part of the budget that we can actually argue about—represented less than a third of what the government spent each year. In 2020, when I began taking management jobs in the Pentagon and really started to pay attention to the budget, just over half of discretionary spending, about 16% of the total annual budget, was spent on the military. *All of the rest of the things we argued about, all year every year*—transportation, housing, education—was just under 15% of the total budget. The other 69% represented the so-called *mandatory* spending that was not subject to debate or adjustment. This included Social Security, Medicare, Medicaid, and something called 'income security' that was really just a euphemism for unemployment payments and federal welfare programs. Another large and growing part of mandatory spending was interest on the national debt. In fact, here you go," he said, handing me a business card with a pie chart on it. "I used to pass these out by the handful, trying to let taxpayers know where their money was going."

FEDERAL BUDGET

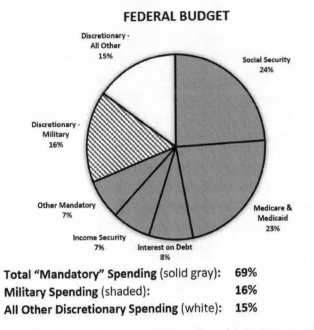

Discretionary - All Other 15%

Social Security 24%

Discretionary - Military 16%

Other Mandatory 7%

Income Security 7%

Interest on Debt 8%

Medicare & Medicaid 23%

Total "Mandatory" Spending (solid gray):	**69%**
Military Spending (shaded):	**16%**
All Other Discretionary Spending (white):	**15%**

Iron George spent the bulk of his Senate career talking about debt. In particular, he questioned the conventional wisdom that "mandatory" spending was truly mandatory. "Setting aside the question of whether the Constitution actually permits the federal government the authority to establish retirement programs for citizens, which it does not," he said in 2032, *"we simply don't have the money."* He became infamous for using terms such as "intergenerational transfer payments" – a professor's term for "borrowing from your grandkids"—to describe how Social Security was not really a savings program for the elderly, but was instead a Ponzi scheme in which money was taxed away from current workers and paid to retirees. This was morally questionable under any circumstances, but the current demographic trends made the collapse of this system inevitable: families were having fewer children, and retirees were living longer. Attempts to balance the ledger by either lowering benefits or raising the retirement age were politically undoable, but this didn't stop George from trying. "Those ideas flew like a lead balloon," he laughed.

As troublesome as Social Security was becoming, the situation with Medicare and Medicaid was even worse, with the federal government getting more involved every year through increasing regulation and the Affordable Care Act. "From the time I was born (in 1981) until 2020, the portion of the U.S. Gross Domestic Product devoted to health care grew from 8% to 17%. Not only were demands for services rising, the use of federal standards for insurance reimbursement meant that the overall costs could continue to grow several times faster than inflation. "It's an iron law of economics," George said on the Senate floor, "anything you subsidize, you'll get more of." It was this speech, along with his success as a debater, that prompted his Senate friends to nickname him "Iron George."

The U.S. depended upon two crutches to prop up its overspending: the authority to print its own money, and the ability to borrow. Despite what the now thoroughly discredited advocates of "Modern Monetary Theory" claimed, a government that simply printed money to solve its fiscal problems would only create more harmful inflation. "Thankfully, politicians and the federal reserve had the good sense to avoid *that*," George sighed, "but it was a pretty popular idea for a while." The other crutch, borrowing through the sale of government bonds, seemed to be an endless fountain of money. Congress routinely raised the debt ceiling every year until 2036 when China decided to stop buying U.S. debt. Congress raised the debt ceiling that year, too, but nobody was buying U.S. debt anymore. "Imagine trying to run a house, but every year you spend more than you make," George argued during the 2033 debt ceiling debate. "Long before the collectors start calling and you get letters warning of foreclosures, banks will stop loaning you money. It's going to happen to the U.S. someday."

✳ ✳ ✳

The debt was a huge problem, and threatened to ultimately sink the United States. What was truly sad, however, was the *dependency* created by programs *funded by debt*. People began to find it perfectly acceptable to demand things from the federal government *first*, instead of either obtaining them on their own or seeking relief from more local entities.

"When I was in college," George said, "one of the few non-socialist professors I encountered talked about the difference between *liberty* rights and *claim* rights. Liberty rights are those enshrined in the Constitution, which places limits on federal power and grants the associated *liberty* to the people. It's not a coincidence that the Bill of Rights is worded in a fashion similar to the Ten Commandments, and that the concept of "thou shalt not" features prominently in each. In addition to the more well-known amendments which prohibit the federal government from interfering with speech, religion, or the right to bear arms, the oft-overlooked Ninth and Tenth Amendments *explicitly forbid* the federal government from encroaching on areas not mentioned in the Constitution. The states and the people retained the right, the *liberty*, to exert any authority not expressly written into the Constitution.

"*Claim* rights, in contrast, are when an individual or group asserts a claim for some benefit. The language of these discussions was pernicious and deliberate, as one group after another claimed a 'right' to health care, a 'right' to housing, a 'right' to higher education, etc. Advocated most strongly by the political left, what these assertions of claim rights overlooked was that each of these so-called rights —housing, health care, and higher education—were actually *products*. Sure, many people regard them as essential products; but others may not.

"For example," he continued, "I could drive just outside of town and see how some people would rather spend money on sports cars instead of their dilapidated houses. I personally know people who have season tickets to the Broncos but who will never go to the doctor, and others who will buy their kid a sailboat but won't pay for the kid's college. Sports cars, season tickets, and sailboats are all products; but should they be a 'right'? How would that be morally any different from housing, health care, and higher education? 'Because we need those things to live,' the left said. *No, clearly you don't...you just want them very badly, and you'd prefer that other people pay for them.* Each of these things—health care, housing, higher education—requires the investment, intellectual energy, and effort of other people to create that product. If you are a doctor, I can no more claim a right to the fruits of your labor than I can claim the right to a Ford Mustang or a football ticket. It's an absurd argument, but the advocates of bigger government had already won the day long before I got to the Senate.

"The worst part about all of it," George continued, "wasn't even the enormous and crushing debt problems created by the triumph of 'claim rights.' The saddest result was the destruction of the human spirit—that almost uniquely *American* spirit—of personal responsibility and independence."

George went on to describe how Americans' individual ancestries varied widely, with some American stories beginning with people arriving as willing immigrants, some arriving in chains, and some Native Americans being here from the beginning of recorded time. "My family has all three categories, by the way," he would add. "However, we are without question, culturally and spiritually, a nation of immigrants. Our collective character was in many ways shaped by people who looked at the situation in their home countries and said 'Enough of this. I can do better!' and left for a better life. The immigrants who built and continue to build this country were optimists and innovators, and did not come here for a handout. They came here to work, and to be free. It is a sad legacy that so many of their children and grandchildren have forgotten their example, and expect the government to be the answer to all of their problems.

"By attempting to serve as an all-loving, all-protecting entity, the U.S. government did much more than simply bankrupt itself, it *robbed the working public of its drive to succeed.* The naturally driven had to ask themselves 'why bother' with the extra effort at innovation or investment if the government was just going to seize an increasingly larger portion of their earnings in taxes. The naturally less-driven were even less inclined to work, now that federal programs mostly removed the consequences of not working."

By 2010 these mutually reinforcing trends— growing government, and a relatively shrinking number of workers to support it—were already threatening the system. By 2020, the debt had doubled again and economists were beginning to sound the alarm louder and louder through the 2020's. However, the initial flashpoints for separation turned out not to be purely economic crises, but two political crises that debt helped cause.

CHAPTER 3

Flash Points: Immigration and Subjugation

> *Socialist governments traditionally do make a financial mess. They always run out of other people's money.*

> MARGARET THATCHER

> *Would it not, in that case, be simpler for the government to dissolve the people and elect another?*

> BERTOLT BRECHT

"Tired of talking about debt?" George asked. I wasn't, but he misread my hesitation and said "Good, so am I. Let's talk about policy. People don't *see* debt. They *see* the policies that debt creates." Although the debt problem had been growing for years, and posed an existential threat to the USA, it was not the kind of thing that the average person got excited about. The numbers were so large that people literally could not imagine what a "trillion" really was, and telling them how many laps around the world a $1 trillion stack of $1 bills could make (10) or how many years it would take to spend $1 trillion at a rate of $1 million per hour (decades) did not make the numbers any more real. To most Americans, a debt of $25 trillion wasn't just hard to imagine. It was imaginary.

"The *second* worst thing about spending and debt," George teased, "was that it was the one thing that both political parties could agree upon. They both wanted more of it. Oh, Republican Congressmen complained about it more than their Democratic counterparts, but they spent just as fast. It pains me to say that the last and only President who achieved his goals of shrinking the federal government *and* the federal debt was Calvin Coolidge.

"The *very* worst thing about spending and debt," as his expression took a serious turn, "was the *set of policies it forced us to adopt*." The numbers regarding Social Security had been grim for a long time. Americans were having fewer children, and living longer in retirement. So, there were fewer young people growing up to get jobs and pay taxes —which kept Social Security afloat—and more people demanding ever-rising, inflation-adjusted payments in retirement. As a "closed system", it was unsustainable without advocating higher birth rates (unpopular), raising the retirement age (politically difficult) or lowering the dollar amount of Social Security benefits (politically impossible). However, it was not truly a "closed system," in that extra labor could be imported through immigration, both legal and illegal. "Few Americans realize that the approximately 7.5% they are paying in Social Security and Medicare taxes—what you in the USA still call 'FICA'—was really only about half of what they were paying to keep these two systems afloat. The other half was taken out of their paycheck before they even saw it.

"You call it *payroll tax*," George explained, "as if the employer is paying it; but it's really just part of the overall cost of having you as an employee, and it would *be paid to the employee if the government weren't seizing it*. Both the left and right in the USA had their primary reasons for wanting more immigration—legal and illegal—but a secondary reason for each was that tax receipts, especially those paid by the employer, were reliable ways to keep social programs like Social Security and Medicare afloat. That was the reason why in the New United States of America (NUSA), the payroll tax was one of the first things we got rid of. We wanted people to know exactly how much they were paying for government programs. But I digress...where was I going next...?"

"Immigration?" I asked. "Oh, yes," and he paused for a heavy sigh. "I shouldn't have to say this, but since identity politics isn't completely dead yet, I have to: many of my ancestors, but not all, were immigrants. Immigration is as important to the success of the NUSA as it was to the initial success of the USA. However, we like to make a distinction between immigrants—those whom we welcome here through an established legal process —and *aliens*—those whose first act was to invade our home illegally." Trying to encourage him to talk more about that, I said "Because there are some jobs that Americans just won't do, right?"

I hadn't been trying to bait Iron George (that was rarely a good idea) but his expression turned cold. "I'm glad you said that, Jack" he replied flatly. "Did you ever wonder *why* Americans *won't* do those jobs? I won't hold a seminar on unemployment here, but the short version is that 'unemployment' only measures the number of people without jobs who *are actively looking for one*—not the number of people who've decided, for whatever reason, that they would rather not work, but instead collect unemployment benefits, disability benefits, or other forms of "income security." In the 25 years from 1995 to 2020, the US population grew just over

20%, but the number of 'disabled workers' receiving federal assistance grew by 100%—five times faster. How was this possible? It was possible because we exploited the truly disabled—the ones who genuinely *deserve* assistance in a compassionate society—by using the same label for those who were all too eager to find an excuse not to work. We needed to import more labor—immigrants and aliens—to help pay for their decision, and for the governments' enabling of their sloth. Americans will do whatever it takes to feed themselves and their families, but if the government allows or encourages them to do less, then you have to expect that some will take the easy way out."

I opened my mouth to say something conciliatory, but George smiled and said "Don't worry. I'll forgive you the common misperception about what Americans won't do for work. Besides," he continued, "the 'rather not work' segment of American society was not responsible for the large number of aliens—over 12 million by 2020. The blame for that problem lay squarely at the feet of both political parties, neither of which had anything to gain by controlling the problem, and probably had a lot to lose.

"For the Republican's part, they were not too eager to undermine many of their business-owning supporters by enforcing labor laws—which have long made it illegal to employ aliens. For their part, the Democrats imagined that new immigrants and aliens, especially poor ones, could be easily manipulated by promises of ever-expanding federal benefits. While Democrats rarely said so openly, the contemptible history of the Citizenship USA program in the 1990's—which promised an accelerated path to citizenship combined with voter registration in key states—fully exposed how the Democrat party believed that a permanent underclass was key to its continued electoral success." The result, in the end, was that neither party wanted to fix the problem, and saw advantages in the status quo.

"Did you ever wonder why so many politicians and advocates sought ways to increase the number of unskilled laborers in the USA, regardless of their legal status, but agreed that foreign graduates of American colleges had to be sent home as soon as they graduated?", George continued. "The US Government systematically sought the lower-skilled workers, while just as systematically sending the brightest potential immigrants home. Nobody likes fearing for their job, but the college-educated elites on both sides of the political spectrum made the rules, and kept their jobs safer from competition. It's no wonder that resistance to these policies grew, especially in the blue-collar sectors of our workforce, whose members strongly believed they were losing jobs to immigrant labor."

* * *

Although politicians sought budgetary relief and potential constituents through immigration, it was never going to be enough to keep the government afloat. The election of 2020, despite predictions of calamity by both sides, did not result in any great change. However, the debt continued to rise —standing at nearly $30 trillion by 2024. Although it would be years before the Debt Crisis of 2036, some in Washington were already seeing the need to significantly raise taxes in order to prevent default. With federal spending increasingly being directed toward the urban centers on the coasts, there was strong resistance to higher taxes within the interior states, which saw themselves as being shortchanged. Discussions about broad tax increases— billed as "tax reform" by Democrats and compliant (or frightened) Republicans—were mostly avoided in the run-up to the election of 2024 when, to everyone's surprise, a Republican won the presidency and Democrats ended up in control of both houses of Congress. Democrats, enraged at the outcome which once again saw their party win the popular vote but lose in the Electoral College, revived an old idea: get rid of the Electoral College in order to minimize the influence of states in the interior.

Abolishing the Electoral College—the method of selecting a President enshrined in the Constitution —had been tried before, with proposed amendments to the Constitution popping up several times during the latter half of the 20th century. Recognizing that amending the Constitution was difficult, supporters of the National Popular Vote Interstate Compact (NPVIC) began an effort in 2006 to get around that problem. Under this scheme, states would agree to disregard their own citizens' votes, and award their states' electors to the winner of the national popular vote. The NPVIC was largely ignored from 2008-2016, when its mostly Democratic backers were satisfied with having a Democrat as President; but it regained attention after the election of 2016 when the loser of that election later called for abolishing the Electoral College. (Her dislike for the Electoral College was not strong enough to prevent her from serving as an elector four years later, however.) Luckily, the NPVIC ultimately failed, crushed by a 2022 Supreme Court decision that ruled that a compact by several states could not supersede the Constitution; but that wasn't the end of the issue.

"The results of the 2024 election made a lot of people on the left very angry," George said, "and they took that anger in a new direction—going after the Electoral College again." No longer placing hopes in the NPVIC, Democratic organizers focused their energy (ironically) at the state level. Although the Supreme Court had delivered two decisions upholding a state's right to punish "faithless electors" for failing to reflect the votes of their state—*Ray v Blair* in 1952 and *Chiafalo v Washington* in 2020—

there was, of course, no requirement for such laws to be in place, and there was a strong Democrat-funded push to repeal state laws that bound electors to vote according to the citizens of their state. They achieved moderate success, in that many more states adopted a proportional scheme for distributing electors, instead of the "winner take all" method that had been the norm in most states.

"What it all came down to," said George, "was an erosion of the power of states. We forgot that this was supposed to be a Republic, in which the various states would have voices of their own. We were too large—and remain too diverse—to be a true nation, in which one set of rules is appropriate for everyone in all circumstances." The effort to abolish the Electoral College, while not completely successful, certainly eroded its influence, and thereby eroded the influence of many states in selecting a president.

"Proponents of abandoning the College, mostly Democrats, argued that 'why should states with a minority of the population have such a large voice?' Did you know that in 2020, Los Angeles County had a higher population than all but ten states? Did you know that, at the same time, the New York/Newark area had more people than all but four states? When a country is ruled from afar by its elites concentrated in small areas on each coast, that's not a republic, that's not even a democracy. That's an *empire*, and the interior resented it."

* * *

"Altogether, what politicians in Washington were trying to do was disassemble the Republic that they were charged with protecting," George continued, "and replace it with a nation more amenable to their interests, and that would bow more rapidly to their demands. Democracy was supposed to be slow, so no one party could move quickly enough to 'fix' a problem for one group by depriving some other group of their fundamental rights or property. The government found the electorate's resistance to their polices terribly inconvenient."

The pressure began to grow significantly in 2024, accelerated in 2033, and became explosive by 2036. Once again fashionable, the term "Socialism" was embraced unapologetically by its supporters. "Socialists always have to resort to tyranny to get people to do what they want, because it's the only way to get someone to work for the state's benefit instead of their own," George continued, "but the first thing they try is taxation. Confiscatory taxation won't work for long without tyranny, however, because a free people will always find a way to avoid taxes; and that's exactly what happened." Starting in 2025, Congress again and again attempted to raise taxes. Although the most severe proposals were vetoed by the Republican president, incremental raises were enough to prompt tax evasion, especially on the coasts, where a service-oriented economy and ready access to politicians made it easier to hide money from tax collectors. If a politician couldn't be persuaded to write a tax break into law, it was possible to move money around in overseas subsidiaries in order to avoid taxes.

"In the interior, it wasn't so easy to 'outsource' the family farm, or a small business on Main Street, so small business owners, farmers, and laborers in medium-sized businesses were stuck paying higher and higher taxes. More separation between coasts and interior. More resentment. More pressure. Somewhere in the middle of all this," George said, "I was dumb enough to accept an appointment to the Senate."

CHAPTER 4

From Policy to Proposal

*What limited people's thinking, and
what allowed government to persist
with incremental seizures of liberty
for so long, was the same thing: the
myth of permanence. Can you name
one other country that has had the
same government for over 200 years?*

GEORGE ERIKSON

INTERVIEW

JUNE, 2046

By 2025, George Erikson had grown tired of the Pentagon. He had just been whiplashed through another post-election changing-of-the-guard, and was beginning to believe that instead of making progress over time, the Department of Defense would just be pretending to re-invent itself every two, four or eight years, depending upon which party fared best in the most recent election. "Although it would have been nice to believe that 'national defense' would be a non-partisan issue, even I wasn't that naïve. What I failed to grasp was just how shameless and money-grubbing the whole appropriations process was—in DoD and elsewhere—and it just turned me off. Every day, I felt less like I was serving my country, and more like I was serving someone's political agenda." Besides, he had never quite "fit" in the capital area—with so many transient people who weren't from there but worked for the government—and he longed to go home.

Home for George Erikson was Laramie, Wyoming. Although his mother had retired from the University of Wyoming years before, George still knew enough people at the University to interview for, and obtain, a position as an adjunct professor of political science. "I loved teaching. It was the happiest time of my life. I felt like I was channeling much of my parents teaching into the classroom; talking about policy in a civil manner. I felt like I was really connecting with my students—many of whom were very young, but there were also some graduate students that had some significant life experience. Then, I had to go and make the mistake of impressing a graduate student that ended up becoming a Senator."

Most are familiar with the story of how Senator Julia Gordon, diagnosed with advanced breast cancer during the first year of her term, bravely recommended to Wyoming Governor Cheryl Davis that Erikson be considered for her replacement in the Senate. Initially skeptical, Davis was impressed with Erikson's approach to problems. "He had a way of speaking that came across as honest and thoughtful," she was later quoted as saying. "His secret—something few politicians were able to understand—was *actually being* honest and thoughtful. He also had this unusual habit of saying 'I don't know' if that was the truth, and of remaining silent until he thought through what he was going to say. I can see why students loved him for it, and why political opponents found it infuriating."

George Erikson was formally appointed to the Senate on October 15th, 2031, agreeing to serve the remainder of Warren's term. Despite working diligently and never missing a vote, *Senator* Erikson summed up his accomplishments in the nation's highest deliberative body in a single word: "unremarkable". "I found it shocking how little I was able to achieve," he told me. "I voted on the losing side against every tax increase. I watched the power of state governments continue to erode in the face of growing federal power. I couldn't even get a debate, much less a Democrat co-sponsor, for a proposed bill on congressional term limits," he recalled. "On the other hand, I was able to start the Blue Sky Group."

Now known to most Americans, the informal think tank known as the Blue Sky Group (BSG) began as a group of Republican senators—and a few sympathetic and discreet Democratic colleagues—from interior states who met weekly for breakfast. "It started as a gripe session," George explained, "a way to vent our frustrations with the growth of government, its indifference to the pain it inflicted on the people, and with the whole political process that dominated more and more of American life while creating very little of value. Each week, it was someone else's turn to play 'what if'. *What if*, for example, we could propose a bill on term limits? What would happen next? What could be the unintended consequences if it passed? That led to some lively and instructive discussions, and we examined a new topic each week.

"The goal, of course, was to generate fresh ideas that could ultimately end up as legislation," George continued. "Well, word about our weekly meetings got into the press, and in that political climate we were immediately branded as a bunch of subversives. We weren't trying to hide anything. We were meeting at Denny's, for crying out loud! Unfortunately, the first thing that happened is that the

BSG became radioactive to our Democratic participants, and they stopped coming to meetings. The second thing that happened was even worse. We actually *became* subversives."

In truth, according to every senator in the BSG that I interviewed, nobody in the group talked about separation from the United States until 2033, when the proposed 28th Amendment to the Constitution—the formal and final abolition of the Electoral College—passed both houses of Congress by the required two-thirds majority. "The influence of electoral votes had eroded significantly over the past decade," George said, "but it still existed as an institution, and still provided some protection against tyranny. My colleagues in the BSG were deeply concerned, which is a fancy way of saying *the 28th Amendment scared the crap out of us*. Our games of 'what if' continued, but the purpose changed. In the beginning, we were just trying to generate ideas for new laws. Now, we were trying to generate ideas for a new country."

❈ ❈ ❈

The policy document generated by the BSG, which continued to meet regularly from 2033-36, formed the core ideas for the New United States of America. Now known as the Blue Sky Declaration, the full text is available to anyone who wants to read it. What follows below are key elements of each policy position, followed by excerpts of my interview with George Erikson.

The Constitution

The Constitution of the New United States of America (NUSA) shall be the Constitution of the United States of America as it existed in the year 2030. It shall come into effect in the NUSA under the conditions outlined in Article VII: the ratification of nine states shall be sufficient for the establishment of this Constitution between the states so ratifying the same.

"Oh, how my friends wanted to tinker with the Constitution!" George began. "To be honest, I was equally tempted, but I knew this would be a disaster. First, our single greatest unifying desire after 2033 was *separation*. We didn't want to 're-invent' America. We wanted to *preserve* America and its Constitution. For all its flaws, the Constitution was how America became great. Sure, it would have been nice to re-write it and eliminate references to slavery, for example, but the temptation this would provide—an open door to every group's "wish list"—would be too much, and separation would never get done. Collectively, we agreed that amendments we believed needed to happen—specifically regarding Congressional term limits—could be dealt with after separation, and that the Ninth and Tenth Amendments could be used more assertively to repeal laws that eroded the influence of the states and the people."

Although he would not admit it to me personally, other members of the Blue Sky Group confided to me that it was Erikson's passionate arguments in favor of retaining the US Constitution that prompted others to view him as the leader of the BSG. When I told him about this, he smiled shyly and said "While it's flattering to hear my friends refer to me as their leader, there were others who just wanted to throw me under the bus in case this didn't all work out.

"Besides," he added, "arguing in favor of the Constitution had several advantages for the movement. First, it was something that members—and the states they represented—could agree upon. Second, it postponed the smaller arguments until later. Instead of trying to create NUSA *and* get everything we wanted at the same time, we could launch the effort to separate and then refine our government at a later date. Finally, it protected us against charges of sedition. After all, we were adopting the exact same government. We were just going to do it over *here*," he said gesturing to one side with his hands, "while the USA did what it wanted over *there*."

Defense

The New United States of America (NUSA), viewing the USA as a natural ally, will enter a mutual defense treaty with the USA.

With the exception of a Coast Guard and Border Patrol, the NUSA will maintain no standing land or air forces trained and equipped for the purpose of deploying outside the NUSA. However, the NUSA will allow its citizens to enlist in the military services of the USA, and to become officers within the same, subject to re-authorization by both houses of Congress and the President of the NUSA every five years beginning in 2040.

Military forces of the USA currently positioned within the borders of the NUSA will be allowed to remain in place, subject to terms of negotiated leasing arrangements similar to those that the USA maintains with other nations.

"As soon as we talked about separation," George began, "fear-mongering reporters and other zealots started drawing 'USA vs NUSA' maps, showing where all the military bases were, and talking about the prospect of a new civil war. It was nonsense.

We were going to *separate from the USA with reluctance*—with the long-term hope that the rest of the USA would eventually come to its senses and join *us*. We knew it would be difficult, but we didn't feel like we had a choice. We certainly didn't want to pick a fight with the USA, and we were confident that they didn't want to pick a fight with us. So, we didn't want an expensive and potentially provocative standing Army and Air Force on our soil. Also, between the USA, Mexico, and Canada, we weren't exactly troubled by aggressive neighbors.

"That said, it would have been immoral to simply depend upon the USA for defense, so we decided that we should allow our citizens to join the armed forces of the USA—personnel they badly needed anyway. In order to prevent NUSA citizens from being sent abroad to pointless or endless wars, however, we wanted to make the participation of NUSA citizens the subject of regular review by the Congress and President of the NUSA. This way, we hoped, the USA would be more judicious than it had been in its use of military force, because we would have a strategic 'veto' over its ability to spend NUSA citizen's lives in ill-considered military adventures.

"The most interesting part, oddly enough, turned out to be basing rights. The number of bases that the USA decided to close instead of pay rent for surprised a lot of people, but not me. I had seen Congressmen in the USA fight tooth and nail to keep bases in their districts open, even those which the Department of Defense said it no longer needed. Once these bases were inside the NUSA, however, the political incentives for those same Congressmen evaporated, and they did not object at all to the closures. In the end, the DoD prevailed upon Congress to keep most of the major facilities open —air and naval bases, in particular—and negotiating with the USA for leasing rights turned out to be easier than expected. Sure, with fewer bases, we had a little less leasing revenue than some of us had expected, but that was a small price to pay for a smooth transition."

Borders And Immigration

In order to enhance the alliance with the USA, and to ensure the greatest liberty to its citizens, the New United States of America (NUSA) shall allow free passage of goods, services and citizens between itself and the USA, for as long as the USA provides the same privileges to the goods, services and citizens of NUSA.

Illegal immigration, or the infiltration of alien labor in to the NUSA, will henceforth be mitigated principally at the point of employment.

"We knew that trade would be vital to our new

nation, so the free movement of people and goods was essential in any case." There was also the moral problem of separating families, George explained. "We all have relatives all over the country. We did not want to create barriers for families, and it was pretty simple for all of us to agree on that."

"Border security, on the other hand, was a much longer argument." While some preferred to have walls and an enormous border force to prevent illegal labor migration, the sheer size of the NUSA-USA border made this expensive and impractical. "Besides, as our history with Mexico had proven," George continued, "these efforts had a limited impact. Border forces would instead be focused on the things that they were best at—intelligence collection, countering smuggling and human trafficking, and other crime-fighting activities in cooperation with federal and local law enforcement.

"The best way to combat the illegal flow of labor would be to reduce the demand for it," George continued. "If aliens could not find jobs in NUSA due to enforcement of existing labor laws, then the flow of illegal labor to fill those jobs would dry up. Of course, that's exactly what happened." Indeed, the rapid growth of the six-year-old NUSA economy had, by the time of this writing, led to the rapid growth of legal and regulated immigration to a degree that the USA never had—with much of this labor coming from the USA itself.

Currency

In order to facilitate trade with the USA, the standard currency within the NUSA will be the U.S. Dollar. The NUSA shall not create any new currency without the consent of two-thirds of each house of Congress within the NUSA.

Historically, new nations don't have much luck with issuing their own currency. The temptation to ease growing pains by printing more money often proves too great, which then leads to inflation and —if they're lucky—the adoption of foreign currencies that have retained their value. There were those within the leadership of NUSA who wanted the NUSA to issue its own currency but were persuaded against this, mostly by George Erikson. "First of all, it was just another darn thing to argue about, and we had enough of those. Second, we already had a stable, in-demand currency: the US dollar. Giving that up for a new currency that could prove worthless would not inspire investor confidence in the NUSA. Lastly, but most importantly, a new currency would have been a barrier to trade with the USA, and we knew we would depend upon that trade. The U.S. dollar is used as a primary currency all over the world. Why not keep it in NUSA? While we asserted the right to print our own currency, it would have been foolish. I thank God that we didn't."

Social Programs

The Congress of the NUSA shall pass no law guaranteeing the provision of income, housing, or health care to any citizen.

The Congress of the NUSA shall not prevent any member state legislature from passing laws providing assistance to the mentally and physically disabled, orphaned children, or others deemed unable by that state legislature to provide for their own well-being.

"In any compassionate society," George began, "there is a collective responsibility to care for the truly ill, the truly disabled, and the truly unfortunate. The NUSA must, and does, have a way to take care of these people. As a nation, however, the guiding principle for the vast majority of the population —those who are not ill, disabled, or unfortunate—is *individual responsibility*. It is not the federal government's job to look after people, ensure they have income, housing and medical care. If a State wanted, it could establish programs to look after its less fortunate residents, and programs at this level would be far less wasteful than a federal program—which on average would take a dollar in taxes in order to deliver fifty cents worth of services.

"What we worried about the most," George said, "was Social Security. As it turned out, we shouldn't have worried so much. We were afraid that people —especially older people—would reject the idea of a *new* country because their retirement income, namely Social Security, was tied to the *old* country. Sure, they knew they could move from NUSA to USA and retain their Social Security benefits without a problem; but we didn't want that. We wanted NUSA to be a home for everybody, and we wanted their wisdom and their talent. There were three other reasons we need not have worried, but we didn't know that in 2036.

"First, according to two large surveys conducted in 2037 and '38, nobody under age 50 was expecting to ever see a Social Security check anyway. The system had been publicly regarded as bankrupt for so long, most workers just viewed the 'FICA' line on their pay stub as just another tax—not money that they were ever going to see again. So, for a majority of workers, it was not a politically sensitive issue to cancel a program that they didn't believe in anyway. Second, we had a good plan, and hired a public relations firm to put the word out:

(a)   Any citizen of NUSA of any age could immediately "opt out" of Social Security. Citizens under age 50 would be disenrolled and no longer pay FICA or have payroll taxes withheld from their paychecks.

(b)   Any citizen of NUSA age 50 or older could continue with Social Security, but with reduced benefits and a higher retirement age (70 instead of 65).

(c)   For those already receiving benefits, payments would be subject to a means test and would no longer be increased on an annual basis.

"Third and finally, we started a public awareness campaign that told people something they should have realized all along: *Social Security is a terrible investment*, and they will be much better off if they save and invest for their own retirement. The average annual return for a medium-to-low risk portfolio of stocks, bonds and savings certificates— something you can buy with a click of a button— was about 5%. If you wanted to play it even safer with only bonds and savings certificates, you could earn 2-3%. Under Social Security, the average return on 'investment' (seizure through taxes) was *one percent*! You would never buy this investment if it was a financial product, but the government of the USA was forcing its citizens to buy it through their taxes."

Debt

The Congress of the NUSA assumes no responsibility for the debts of the government of the USA.

States which become part of the NUSA--either as an original member state or later through later accession--will not be relieved of their debts by the government of the NUSA.

"We never declared war on anybody, and most likely never will; but there were some in the USA that thought this came pretty close," George explained. "The government of the USA was furious that they should be 'hung out to dry', as they were fond of saying, by being held solely responsible for their own debt. They even blamed us for China's decision to stop buying U.S. Treasury Bills in 2036, and it seemed like a logical argument at the time. We know now, however, that the Chinese had been considering that move for at least a decade, had long been worried about the risk of US default on its debt, and were playing 'what if' games of their own."

I asked George why didn't the NUSA go farther and pass an amendment to the Constitution requiring that annual federal budgets be balanced, as had been proposed by President Ronald Reagan in the 1980's. "Some were against it because they didn't believe that a new Republic needed a 'fiscal straight-jacket'—a legal restraint on its spending—right out of the gate, and some just didn't think it would pass. I would have loved to place the new federal government in a fiscal straightjacket, because it was *debt* that got us into this mess in the first place. However, I had to agree that a balanced budget amendment wouldn't have passed in that political climate. Arguing about that would have just slowed down the launch of NUSA, and proponents of a balanced budget amendment, like me, just decided to add it to our "wish list" for after 2040.

Accession

Once ratified by the conventions of at least nine states as outlined in Article VII of the Constitution, the Constitution of the New United States of America (NUSA) shall become the law of the land within the borders of those states.

Member states of the United States of America (USA) may join NUSA as whole states, provided both a majority vote in that State's legislature and a majority vote in a statewide referendum so approve.

Portions of member states of the USA may join a contiguous member state of the NUSA, provided that (a) a majority of USA citizens within the affected territory approve by referendum, and (b) a majority of the legislature of the gaining NUSA state approves, and (c) a majority of both houses of the Congress of NUSA approves.

"Remembering that the long-term goal was to save America, not merely secede from it, we had to have a way for states to join us, and we didn't want to make it difficult. We also didn't want to create havoc in the USA by having segments of states breaking away pell-mell, so we made it more difficult, but still possible, for a *portion* of a state to do that. In short, we wanted to make it easier for our neighbor states to join us, but we wanted to be good neighbors to the states that did not."

* * *

By 2036, the debt crisis was at a boiling point, exacerbated greatly by China's decision to stop purchasing US government debt through treasury bills —which meant that nobody would buy US debt anymore. Two other things happened that quickly turned the debt crisis into a political crisis. First, the 28th Amendment abolishing the Electoral College was ratified, making it so that the President of the USA would be selected by the national popular vote. "We feared that this would mean the President of the United States would now be the *President of a Few Large Cities*," George sighed. Second, the Democratic party swept the Presidency, Senate and House of Representatives later that year; having run on a platform of increased social programs for cities on the coasts and increased taxes for everyone.

"At the next meeting of the BSG, nobody talked," George said quietly. "We had spent nearly three years talking about separation from the USA, but in the wake of three overlapping events that would seem to push us in that direction—the Debt Crisis, the abolition of the Electoral College, and looming tax increases—nobody had anything to say. The truth is, we were all terrified. Finally, Senator Kirk Browning from Texas asked 'Is it time?'"

George grew quiet. "I didn't want this. Nobody did. It was the best outcome available for a terrible situation. People who were *politically* disenfranchised were now expected to provide *economic* support to the people who had denied them their rights. It just couldn't happen anymore. We were either going to separate, or explode."

On New Year's Day, 2037—just days before new Congress was going to be sworn in—the last Republican-led Senate in the United States of America passed a one-sentence resolution calling for state legislatures to consider the question of separation according to the terms of the Blue Sky Declaration. "I held up the document briefly during my remarks, but had to set it back down on the podium," George confided. "My hands were shaking."

CHAPTER 5

The Challenge

> When I joined the Air Force, I took an oath that I reaffirm today: "I, George Erikson, do solemnly swear that I will support and defend the Constitution of the United States against all enemies, foreign and domestic; that I will bear true faith and allegiance to the same; that I take this obligation freely, without any mental reservation or purpose of evasion, so help me God."
>
> GEORGE ERIKSON
>
> THE CHEYENNE DEBATE
>
> OCTOBER, 2037

"The first thing I want you to know about President Franklin Harris," George said sternly, "was that he was and remains a decent man. He said a few things in that debate that he regretted later, but he never got personal." When a newly inaugurated President first challenged *former* Senator Erikson to a debate over the Blue Sky Declaration in April 2037, he was stunned by the response—or lack of it.

"I ignored him," George said flatly. "I was done with politics. As everyone knew when I agreed to take the Senate job in 2031, I was not going to run for re-election. I had barely moved anything into my one-bedroom apartment in Washington, DC, and happily packed up five years later; after the Blue Sky Declaration on January 1st, 2037. When I heard about President Harris's challenge, I was already back in my old office at the University of Wyoming, and I wasn't even going to consider going back east just to argue. I had done my part, said what I had to say, and I was going to go back to teaching. Besides, Harris was a bit late. The question of separation had already been taken up by twelve state legislatures by March 2037, and it looked like more states were going to join them.

"Also, while I was not a professional politician, I knew a setup when I saw one," George continued. The movement to separate was rapidly gaining momentum, and what the leadership in the USA needed was something to slow it down. If they could set up and then knock down a 'straw man'—me—they hoped it would deflate the movement, and I did not want to give them that chance. The movement was never supposed to be about *me*, anyway. It was supposed to be about freedom, about ideas."

The text of the debate is available to all, and neither a full-text rendering nor a blow-by-blow analysis is necessary here. What is worth exploring, however, is George Erikson's thoughts and motivations leading up to the debate, and some of his perspectives as a participant. "The most remarkable thing to me, at the time, was that the President wanted to debate on this subject at all. I had underestimated how strong the political pressure was on him. He did not want to be the President who presided over the separation of the nation; but I'm glad he was. He wasn't a hothead. Sure, he got flustered during the debate. That would have been hard to avoid because, the poor man, the facts just weren't on his side."

Another thing that surprised observers at the time was the setting. Many thought that as soon as the President agreed to a debate in Cheyenne, Wyoming that he had already lost an important "image point" by going out of his way to debate Erikson on his turf. "How did you manage to negotiate that?" I asked. George laughed. "I didn't negotiate at all. After ignoring two more calls for a debate over the summer of 2037, I responded to a third by saying 'no thank you, I have no intention of leaving Wyoming for any reason, and certainly not to argue with a President.' Once again, I had underestimated the political pressure he was under. By then, seven states had already opened conventions to ratify a new Constitution under the principles of the Blue Sky Declaration, and five more conventions were scheduled to begin before the end of the year. I imagine Harris was genuinely concerned for his country, and supremely concerned about his legacy. Losing half your territory doesn't look good on a presidential resume. Then one day in September, I walked out of my office to find my graduate assistant looking unusually pale. 'You have a call from the White House.'"

"My colleagues and co-authors in the Blue Sky Group—a mix of sitting and former senators—were thrilled," George recalled. "But I was terrified. The movement I had helped create was well under way, and I did not see anything to gain—and saw everything to lose—by going on television and potentially messing this all up. But there it was, an invitation to a televised debate at eight PM on a Wednesday night at the Cheyenne Civic Center— roughly three weeks from the White House phone call. I called in a few colleagues to help prepare, put them up at a local hotel, and we figured out how to approach the issue. *Should we go on offense? Should we let the President go on offense?* Some thought this was the best strategy: let the President 'punch himself tired' and appear to be the aggressor. I didn't think so. While I did not know Harris well, he had just won the Presidency, and even in a lopsided election that was no easy feat. He was probably pretty good at offense, and I guessed that he didn't easily get tired."

The first thing the re-convened BSG did was reply to the President's invitation by agreeing to a debate at seven PM instead of eight. "We were immediately accused of trying to maximize our television audience on the east coast," George laughed, "which we recognized as a benefit, but that wasn't the reason. The fact is, I'm normally heading to bed around 8:30pm. Did I mention that I'm boring? The second thing that we did was agree on approach. We were not going to go on 'offense' vs. the USA, but we were not going to let the President punch away at us, either, should he decide to do that. We were going to clearly and forcefully assert our principles and explain, without drowning the audience in detail, the economic and political facts that support those principles."

"How much did you rehearse for the debate?" I asked. "Endlessly," he replied, "and for all that, it was the ad-libs that people remember—the things I never planned on saying until the President said something that prompted me to reply. I knew that I wanted to recite my Oath of Office near the beginning of the debate, to reinforce the point that the NUSA was actually going to be loyal to the Constitution, and so that new observers could see that we weren't anti-American or zealots. I never imagined that the President would quibble with me over the text. I didn't think about my reply at all."

In an event now known to most Americans, George Erikson recited the Oath of Office that he took when joining the U.S. Air Force. President Harris surprised him by replying "You forgot the part about *and that I will well and faithfully discharge the duties of the office which I am about to enter*—which is actually part of the Oath of Office for the President of the United States. Through his quibble, the President inadvertently set, and then walked into, one of the more famous rhetorical traps in history. "No, Mr. President. I don't want your job," Erikson replied. "I want to be free." For an unplanned utterance, the simple phrase "I want to be free" became wildly popular, soon to be found on flags, posters and bumper-stickers all over the states that would become NUSA, and in many states that remain in the USA as well.

"At what point did you realize that you were winning the debate?" I asked. "Well, I never stopped feeling uncomfortable, but when the President replied to my criticism of higher and higher taxes by saying 'The states of your so-called 'movement' represent only a small portion of overall US tax receipts,' I started feeling better about things." To those who may have missed the debate or haven't read the transcripts, Erikson's reply was "That's good news, Mr. President. You won't miss them, then. To us, however, that's a lot of money."

"I got the sense that this rattled him," George explained. "I don't think he hired the right people to help him prepare for the debate, if he did prepare, because for all his good qualities, he didn't seem to imagine that there could be a perspective on separation that was completely different from his own." I asked George if there was anything not in the transcript, not known to the public, about the debate that he could share. "Oh, yes. It was the look in his eye, and his hands.

"When I began a summary statement by saying 'when the New United States of America is born...' Harris interrupted by saying 'You're going to regret it.' It was the only time Harris interrupted me, and I think he immediately recognized his mistake. He'd spoken a bit too fast, and a bit too loud." This moment, now the stuff of debate legend, was when George employed his long-practiced tactic of taking an overly-long time to reply, to stare at an opponent and smile, and lower his voice. "Mr. President, why, exactly, will we regret it?"

"You could have heard a pin drop," George whispered. Harris's blank stare was caught on video, but behind the podium, "His hands were shaking. At that moment, he finally realized what we in the movement had known all along: there was no appetite for use of force in the USA. Harris had made

the mistake of appearing threatening, while simul-
taneously acknowledging through his silence that
there was nothing behind the threat. People on the
coasts called the interior 'flyover country' and took
issue with interior states' intentions to separate;
but in the end, Los Angeles wasn't going to war with
Nebraska just to keep it."

CHAPTER 6

With Friends Like These...

Never underestimate the dangers posed by the wrong friend.

GEORGE ERIKSON

INTERVIEW

JUNE, 2046

At a rare pause, I asked a question. "You've talked about high-level challenges, from President Harris in particular. What were some of your other challenges?" George didn't hesitate. "Morons!" he nearly shouted. "Never underestimate the danger posed by the wrong friend; or in this case, repugnant people *wanting to be* your friend."

It's worth pausing here to discuss George Erikson's attitude about race, as it has strong personal and policy implications for him. He still won't identify himself as a member of any particular group, and when prompted to he starts talking about geography. "I don't talk about this much, but my personal story reflects the story of this land. Many of the places around here are named, as I am, after immigrants from Europe. Just to the north, you have the Wind River Indian Reservation, and the land just to the south of here belonged to Mexico until about 200 years ago. From the other direction," he said pointing east, "I have a piece of chain once worn by another ancestor. I am as American as anyone else, and my family's story is reflected in my skin; *but not in my beliefs.* Those, I choose for myself. My political ideas are not driven by a color."

"Perhaps I was naïve," he continued, "but it never crossed my mind that the New United States of America—an idea born as a reaction to surging debt, crushing taxes, and dwindling political rights —would attract or repel anyone based on some imagined racial agenda. The color of the citizenry does not matter. What matters is the values that the people hold dear. NUSA was designed to be, and is, a place where 'maximum freedom of the individual' should reign supreme, tempered only by a respect for the rights of others. However, not long after we got rolling, we began to attract attention from a variety of malcontents who saw us as an answer to their problems with the USA. In truth, their problems weren't with the USA. Their problems were that they were bigots, tax cheats, and crazies —all of whom would have been rejected by any civil society. We didn't want them, either!

"Not only did we believe they would fail to contribute," George continued, "we feared they would become exactly what they became—a lightning rod for critics, mostly from the U.S. Government. NUSA was called a 'proposed haven for white supremacists, tax protesters, and gun nuts.' In the end, this small number of 'supporters' caused us more problems than any of our adversaries. These groups didn't really quiet down until we started talking about repealing the 24th Amendment to the Constitution and requiring people to pay taxes in order to vote in federal elections. They realized that most of their members wouldn't be able to vote in NUSA if that happened." He then dropped his voice to a whisper "We still haven't repealed the 24th Amendment, but don't tell them that."

"Some were downright scary," he continued. "In 2034, militia leaders contacted my Senate office to volunteer the services of their so-called 'armies' to the NUSA. I am a big supporter of citizens' rights to bear arms, but these guys were loonies and I forcefully declined to meet with them. Some were even more despicable, but entertaining. Remember, few people knew what I looked like before 2031 because, as a DoD procurement official and college lecturer, I wasn't exactly 'out there' in the press. Clearly, the 'racial purity' people that approached me as a senator hadn't done their homework either," he laughed. "I even invited a few of them into my Senate office for a picture. I would just grin as wide as I could, savoring how they tried to hide their surprise and discomfort. What I wanted to say was *here, take this back to your racist friends —a picture with 'Senator Brownskin', or 'Senator Mutt' to be more accurate. If you owned a computer, or knew how to use one, you friggin' moron, you would have known...* but I was too busy laughing on the inside to say any of that."

This was the only time I'd seen, or even heard of, George getting even a little bit angry. Seeing the surprise on my face, he immediately apologized and said "I'm sorry. I just despise bigots. Anyone who judges me by the color of my skin—whether they wish me ill, or want to give me a handout—is not someone I have time for. My beliefs are the results of how I was raised, the experiences I have had, and the thoughts I have about them. I will get by on my wits, my will, and my work ethic alone. If you dislike me because of my color, then you've told me all I need to know about you and we don't need to talk. If you think I need help because of my color, well, you're going to get an earful.

"Thankfully, the vast majority of Americans I encounter, both here in NUSA and in the USA, don't care what color I am, if they even think about it at all. What I am even more grateful for," George concluded, "was that the New USA was ultimately able to avoid being associated with unsavory groups that represent only a small fraction of the citizenry; but this took a lot of deliberate effort and communication about our true message."

CHAPTER 7

Ratification and Separation

> *The collective wisdom of the people of the New United States of America, expressed both through their direct votes and the proper influence of their various and elected state governments, will yield better solutions than any committee of experts in the capital.*

GEORGE ERIKSON

SPEECH AT SOUTH DAKOTA STATE UNIVERSITY

MAY, 2040

The years 2038 and 2039 were filled with a blizzard of speculation, anticipation, and worry. Of the twelve states that considered ratification in 2037 and 2038, all twelve had voted in favor of separation. After the first state—Missouri—had chosen January 1st, 2040 as an effective date of separation, the rest had followed suit. While the choice for separation was an answer to the biggest question, there were many more questions that followed. How many states would join? Would the country have a coast? What would the capital of the new nation be?

"In 2038 and '39," George began, "there was a lot of talk about things that 'the talkers' couldn't control. Well-meaning people, from inside *and outside* the territories that would become NUSA, were offering advice and opinions about what policies the 'new nation' should adopt, how big it should be, where the capital should be, etc. I began to worry. *These sorts of decisions will be up to the states*, I kept telling people. Some seemed to forget that we weren't trying to form a 'nation' at all, and that we were trying to *re*-form a united *Republic*. In fact, most of us wanted to use the Ninth and Tenth Amendments to the Constitution to repeal a wide array of legislation that served to nationalize so many policies that should have been left to the states in the first place. I was worried that the tendency to look for solutions at the highest levels of government first, that noxious weed that caused the US government to grow so large throughout the 20th century, was going to take root in NUSA!"

I asked if there were other distractions, other concerns, during the period between ratification and separation in 2040. "Oh, the maps," George replied. "Maps, maps and more maps! The most popular version was the simplified overlay: possible NUSA borders and population, possible NUSA borders and voting trends, etc. There was also the popular *NUSA vs USA* theme, which covered everything from population, natural resources, coastlines, ports, economic activity, etc. At one point I wondered how many amateur cartographers there were in the country, but then I realized that any reporter with an internet connection could create a moderately accurate info-graphic. That, as it turns out, was exactly what was happening: reporters would create a splashy map to headline their story, and then write about the trends as if it was actually news. Interestingly, the story almost always featured some unnamed 'they' who would have to make a decision about the situation in the 'proposed NUSA', as the reporters referred to it then. What was missing from nearly all of these missives was the idea I just spoke about: these decisions would be made by the people of the involved states and their legislatures. These solutions were not going to be dictated by any one person or one governing body.

"There was, however, one set of decisions the

Blue Sky Group felt that we had to weigh in on," George admitted. The BSG had continued to meet in 2038 and 2039, and was formally referring to itself as the Blue Sky *Advisory* Group to emphasize that it did not have any governing authority, despite being made up of mostly sitting senators. "We wanted a long coast, and we needed a capital. Although we anticipated good economic relations with the USA, we did not want to be a landlocked country. While most were pretty certain that Alabama, Mississippi and Louisiana would join NUSA as original members, there was quite a bit of worry about Texas and Florida. Despite concerns about the changing political landscape in Texas, I was less worried, and knew that it could provide an answer to both of these questions."

Between his second and third year in college, George Erikson spent a summer working at a cattle ranch in Texas. Lured into the opportunity by his college roommate, and growing weary of long nights in the library studying, he was looking forward to long days of physical labor—and he got what he was looking for. "What I came to appreciate about Texas," he mused, "was the difference between the *caricature* and the *character* of Texas. The caricature—the jokes—were about anything 'big'; that Texans liked their big state, their big belt buckles, and their big hair. People mock the 'Texas accent' but, when you travel the South, you learn the Texas accent is often more subtle than some of the surrounding states. However, the true *character* of Texas, and the people in it, is very interesting. When the state opened up to settlement in the 1800's, many went there, and then left just as quickly. It was a hard life, and the people that stayed there were, by and large, strong, hard-working, fiercely independent and self-reliant. These traits are, not surprisingly, passed onto their descendants. Also, every child in Texas learns about how their state was at one time its own nation, however briefly, and they grow up proud of that history."

"When we were talking about the shape and size of NUSA," George continued, "I thought that Texas, if it could be persuaded to join us, would be a key to our success. Some thought that proposing the capital of Dallas was a political move, something that would help persuade Texas to join. As it turned out, Texas was one of the leaders; being second to ratify by only a day (behind Missouri). It wasn't until later that year, 2038, that we proposed the idea of Dallas serving as the capital. It turned out to be a good choice: strong economy, good airport, good tech infrastructure, and relatively few natural disasters. Having decent sports teams doesn't hurt, either," he laughed.

"Jokes aside," he continued, "serving as the capital of NUSA was not supposed to be a big 'prize.' We did not want the federal government to get that big. Washington D.C., in contrast, had grown exponentially in population and power along with the growth of the federal government. Unfortunately, while DC contained some striking architecture and interesting museums, almost everything else about the city had been a disappointment, with its schools, government and crime rate an international embarrassment.

"This is getting off the subject a bit," George prefaced, "but thinking ahead, when the rest of the states join NUSA, which I believe they will, I hope that the government of NUSA will make it a condition of entry that the remaining part of the District of Columbia be returned to the state of Maryland, just like the southern portions of the capital district were returned to Virginia in 1846. It would be nice if Washington could also return to being the capital of a fifty-state NUSA; but it should never have been a separate political entity of its own, and making it one again would lead to the same problems of neglect and corruption that plagued the citizens of that city. Making it a federal district broke one of Aristotle's basic tenets: *that which is owned by all is cared for by no one.* The management and funding of the city should be left to the city itself and an elected state government, not a federal government elected by people who don't live there. The buildings of the federal government can remain federal property, just like the government holds federal property in other cities and states."

Returning to the subject of the interim period between ratification and separation, I asked George if there were any missed opportunities or regrets. He remained silent an unusually long time, as if considering whether or not to tell me something. "I don't have regrets," he began slowly, "but there is one thing I'm not particularly proud of. I guess I ought to come clean about it." He mused further. "Do you remember all the jokes about going to war for 'flyover country?'"

"Oh, yes!" I replied, perhaps a bit too enthusiastically. "*Why fight when you can fly!* and *No war for corn!*" I began to recite a third when his stare cut me short. I slowly closed my mouth and said "I didn't mean any offense, I just..." George cut me off. "No, that's not it. I'm just wondering if I should tell you something. I prefer to be straightforward in all things, but we did one thing—and only one thing—during the entire movement that wasn't completely above board. Maybe I'll just ask you something instead: did you ever wonder who was writing all those jokes?"

Almost apologetically, he went on. "We wanted to win on the intellectual heft of our arguments alone, and we wanted to peacefully separate; but we also knew that there were hotheads on both sides. In the interim period, as I mentioned, there were people drawing *USA vs NUSA* maps. The scarier ones showed where all the missiles and military bases were, and selling—*literally* selling, in books and media--their analysis of how a second civil war would play out. While we considered a NUSA vs USA war very unlikely, it was something we didn't want. Truthfully, the imbalance of power meant there would have been no 'war', per se, but rather a military occupation of the NUSA by the USA. We didn't have the means to resist that, either.

"Even if you set aside the absurdly dangerous notion of taking command of federal forces located in NUSA states," George continued, "*we didn't want to challenge the USA*. We wanted a peaceful separation; to keep part of the nation afloat until the rest of it could come to its senses and join us. Defiant rhetoric would have only played into the hands of the hotheads."

So, instead of daring the USA to use force—which would have been unforgivably foolish—a few members of the Blue Sky Advisory Group quietly set about making a joke of the idea of going to war; at one point even hiring a comedian to ghost write one-liners and riddles. Many of these jokes revolved around the central theme of a brief USA vs NUSA conflict, with the USA being the unhappy "winner" of places like Iowa. However, once the "not worth a fight" genre of joke gained popularity in the USA, comedians and pundits of all types were happy to add their own. It was a genuine reflection of how the vast majority of people in the USA felt about the issue, but Erikson's people just gave it a little boost. Looking down at his hands, George smiled wryly and admitted "It was the only sneaky thing we did.

I should probably feel guilty about it, but I don't. I feel more guilty about picking on Iowa—a truly beautiful place—than about being the ghost writer of jokes that promoted peace."

There was another much-discussed question at the birth of the New United States of America: who would be the President? "Members of the BSG started joking with me about that in 2035," George said. "When Senator Browning from Texas called me in 2039, and told me that the old membership had asked him to approach me about running for President of NUSA as a Republican, I knew that it wasn't a joke anymore. I didn't have anything prepared to say, so I think I said something profound and historic like 'Nope. No way. Sorry.'

"Later on, when the Democrats made *their* pitch to have me lead their ticket for President, I was slightly more elegant, quoting George Washington's line about my fear that 'my countrymen will expect too much of me.' Few people realize how apprehensive Washington was about becoming President," he continued. "Despite his accomplishments, he remained a humble man, and was wise enough to realize that people's very high expectations of him might lead them to be disappointed in him later."

"The truth is, I'm a thinker, a teacher, and maybe, if I really stretch myself, a bit of a visionary," Erikson continued. "If people ask me, I'll be happy to offer my opinion, and as a citizen of NUSA I retain that right in any case. However, I'm not a politician. I've never run a large organization, and I believed that there were better people for the job in NUSA. Turns out, I was right. I am proud of a lot of things about my new country, and one of them is that we've already had two orderly elections in 2040 and '44, and one peaceful transition of power. I'm also proud that we have two strong parties—the Democratic and Republican parties of NUSA—that provide avenues for people to express themselves politically. I've made no secret of the fact that my personal philosophies lead me to agree more with Republican policies than Democrat policies most of the time; but I know many Democrats loyal to the Constitution, and a one-party state would not have been healthy for the Republic."

CHAPTER 8

Rebirth and Refinement

> *Unlike the American Revolution, the birth of the New United States of America was not a "shot heard 'round the world." It was really more like the click of a computer mouse, or the starting of a delivery truck.*

GEORGE ERIKSON

INTERVIEW

JUNE, 2046

Although the New United States of America was born on January 1st, 2040, it was born neither whole nor perfect. Depending upon one's perspective, New Year's Eve 2039 was filled with anticipation, excitement, sadness, or worry. "I had a variety of thoughts on the eve of separation," George started. "Sure, I was excited. I had been thinking, writing, and speaking about this for years. I was also a little sad that it had come to this. I would have preferred that the USA come to its senses regarding outrageous debt and incremental seizures of liberty decades ago; but that ship had sailed, and I had no regrets or second thoughts about splitting away. I believed, and still believe, that this situation of *two USAs*—old and new—will be temporary.

"As for worries, I had few. The birth of the New USA was not the calamity that some expected, and was nowhere near as stressful a time as the birth of the USA. Unlike the American Revolution, the birth of the New United States of America was not 'a shot heard 'round the world'. It was really more like the click of a computer mouse, or the starting of a delivery truck; but people in the USA heard those sounds and liked them. While the NUSA had a healthy economy all its own, we hoped that our lower taxes and smaller government would attract business from the USA. We had no idea what a flood it would be! Within fifteen months the Treasury was flush; partially because of new businesses, partially because our new federal government wasn't spending much.

"The amateur cartographers," George continued, "finally had their first *real* maps in 2040, showing 12 contiguous states and a long, beautiful coast that included Texas, Louisiana, Mississippi and Alabama." The counties on the Florida panhandle had wanted to separate from Florida and join the NUSA on January 1st also, but once the Florida legislature called for a convention on ratification, these counties were persuaded to wait and join with the rest of their state. Florida was the first state to complete the accession process, in July 2042; but the mapmakers kept busy. By the end of 2044, nine more states—including Alaska and the coastal states of Georgia, South Carolina, and North Carolina—had held conventions and joined NUSA. Idaho, Montana and Utah joined in 2045.

When asked what state he thought would be number twenty-six to join the NUSA, George said "I don't want to jinx it, but I'm hoping Washington. There is a dispute between coastal and interior—between Seattle and Spokane—but Seattle is going broke from businesses leaving for NUSA. I would like to see the state join us while it still has some remnants of its former economy, so I believe and hope they will join us next. If Washington doesn't join us, we'll consider the first accession of a partial state—East Washington.

"Another bad thing that didn't happen," George

said, changing subjects, "was the dollar collapse." As the reader probably knows, the USA formally defaulted on its debt in 2043, not long after Florida joined NUSA. However, the strength of the NUSA economy, which also used the dollar, was such that the currency was still in demand, and did not decrease in value even after the USA defaulted. "The smartest thing we did was *not* exercise our right to create our own currency," George repeated. "As I mentioned, this allowed us to use a stable currency and trade easily with the USA. Another benefit was that we knew, or at least hoped, that states of the USA would join us. We wanted them to join us with healthy economies intact, but we knew that many of them would be under fiscal strain. The pain for them was reduced by the fact that their debt default did not also lead to their currency plummeting in value and economic collapse. So, part of the reason we didn't print our own money was to be good neighbors, while another part was purely self-interest. We wanted to absorb new states that were economically as healthy as possible."

* * *

After separation, there was still a lot of work to be done. "The biggest challenge," George began, "was dialing back the 'Good Idea Machine': the tendency to want to tinker with everything in a continuous effort to 'improve' every aspect of society instead of sticking to the basics. I did not want the government of NUSA to be particularly active. There were some early arguments, but I was happy to see that the government did not lose sight of what it was *not allowed to do*, and became the restrained government that allowed for the 'liberty rights' that I spoke about earlier. I actually advocated that legislative sessions should convene alternately, with one session allowed to consider *new* legislation, with a following session focused on *repealing existing* legislation. I didn't get my way on that one, but enough legislative committees were active in the 'repeal and replace' movement that led to a streamlining of regulation and greater transparency in government."

Partially because of the influence of George Erikson, and partially because these initiatives were naturally in harmony with the founding ideals of NUSA, three amendments to the Constitution of NUSA were passed between 2041 and 2044. They are listed below, with Erikson's comment on each:

1) Congressional term limits—The 28th Amendment:

"This had been a popular idea for a long time in the USA, and ideally should have become law the same time as Presidential term limits in the 1940's; but asking Congressmen to turn off their own 'personal wealth machine' was like asking a lion to give up an antelope carcass. We knew this was going to get more difficult with each passing year in the

NUSA, so we jumped on this right away. Now, some-one can only serve three terms in the House for a total of six years, and two terms in the Senate for a total of 12 years. Our founding fathers did not envision a class of lifelong, professional politicians; and in the NUSA this can no longer happen in Congress. The longest that any one person can serve in Congress is 18 years."

2) Fixing the number of Supreme Court Justices at nine—The 29th Amendment:

"Americans were reminded again in 2020, and then again in 2036, that the US Constitution did not fix the number of judges on the Supreme Court. Threats to 'pack the court' with judges friendly to the majority party's agenda didn't have to be carried out to have a chilling effect on judges' impartiality. If the Court was just going to be a rubber stamp on the President's or the Congressional majority's opinion, then there was no point in having a third branch of government. It was time to end this threat, and fix the number of Supreme Court Justices at nine."

3) Repeal of the 17th Amendment –The 30th Amendment:

"While the direct election of senators seemed like a good idea at the time, it tragically undermined the role of the States—which America's founding fathers believed should influence the federal government through their legislatures' selection of senators. This tragedy was punctuated by farce in that the Senate—which was envisioned to be a more senior body of wiser statesmen, less vulnerable to the passions of the people than their counterparts in the House—had instead become a clown show full of camera-hawks and glory-seekers, with all the inflamed passions (or pretend passions) of the House but with more fraud, deceit and permanence.

"This amendment was a harder sell than term limits or fixing the size of the Supreme Court, but when we reminded people that they still *choose the legislature that chooses the senators*, and incorporated a mechanism for the people to recall a senator by popular vote, the amendment passed easily. We got exactly what we hoped for, a Senate that acted in accordance with its original purpose: to review legislation, and to think *long term*; not just another body of politicians that thought up new ways to spend money."

* * *

"What remains to be done?" I asked. George thought about that for probably two minutes, which seemed like a long time. It was getting late in the day, and I feared that he was about to declare the interview over. "Not much," he said. "As a framework, the government of NUSA was pretty solid even before the 28th, 29th, and 30th Amendments.

After all, it was the same Constitution that carried the USA through more than two centuries. What was different about NUSA was that we re-embraced the founding principle that the *federal government should do less*. So, more tinkering probably isn't necessary.

"I suppose if I had a wish list," he continued, "I would pass a balanced budget amendment—making it illegal to spend more in a given year than what is collected in tax receipts. The problem is, if the government is confronted with an emergency, this sort of amendment places a restraint upon government. Sure, one can write a provision to allow deficit spending in an emergency, but then you get into the problem of defining what an 'emergency' is, and the whole argument gets complicated. I would still like to see a balanced budget amendment, but I can live without it.

"For a long time," he continued, "I was interested in repealing the 24th Amendment and making it so that people were required to pay federal taxes—or at least serve the Republic in some capacity—before voting in federal elections; but I have changed my mind on that. Repealing the 24th Amendment falls into the category of ideas that have *intellectual* merit, but are not *practically* wise. Said more simply, on the one hand it makes sense. If you join a garden club, you have to pay dues if you want to vote. Why should a Republic be any different? After all, one of the things that got us in trouble in the

USA was that people who did not contribute to society were still able to vote themselves buckets of other people's money, just as Alexis de Tocqueville warned us in 1835.

"On the other hand," he continued, "repealing the 24th Amendment opens the door to the old poll tax, and the Pandora's box of bad things that could happen if a state tries to disenfranchise a particular group. All in all, I favor leaving the 24th Amendment in place." He smiled, "But it was useful to talk about in those early days, when the white supremacists, tax cheats, and crazies talked about flocking to NUSA, but were turned off when they realized that their inability or unwillingness to pay taxes might mean that they couldn't vote.

"We are a new country," he concluded. "We don't have all the answers yet. However, *we don't have to have all the answers!* The beautiful thing about NUSA is that we once again have a federal government that is *restrained* by our Constitution. That restraint leads to more freedom for the people who, if self-reliance fails, can look to their local and state governments for answers. When an entity— be it a city, county or state—finds a solution that works, other areas can duplicate that success if they choose, or find an even better way to deal with the issue. Except in the areas of foreign affairs, ensuring a stable currency, and promoting free trade, the federal government almost never has the best answer for a problem anyway. The states are once again free to be the 'laboratories of democracy' that they were intended to be."

* * *

By now it was dark, and I wasn't looking forward to the long drive back to Jackson. "I have just one more question," I said. "Do you consider yourself to be the father of a new country, or the savior of an old one?"

"Neither," said George Erikson. "The best you can say for me...'us', really...was that we built a lifeboat. When you start a journey, no one plans to end up in the lifeboat, and nobody wants to. But when the ship is sinking, there's no more welcome sight on Earth.

"We separated from the USA with our hand out in friendship. We wanted, at the very least, to be part-ners—and I think we are. What we hoped for, and are happy to see happening, is that individual states and ultimately the whole USA would join us and we would become one Republic again.

"When the lifeboats are first deployed, some-times denial sets in, and some wish to remain aboard the sinking ship. It's noble, but ultimately futile. When they come to their senses and fully ap-preciate the dire situation they are in, they jump off the ship and get on the lifeboat. That's all that the

New United States of America was ever meant to be: a place where America's founding principles of liberty and self-reliance could once again flourish, and by the exercise of those principles become strong enough to save the rest of the states. We've got a ways to go, but it's working."

AFTERWORD

I have been asked if I hope for the orderly secession described in this book. The answer is no, for
the same reason I do not hope for life-saving surgery: it's not necessary yet. If I ever develop a
life-threatening medical condition, however, I will
probably change my mind about the surgery. What
I hope for is that the growth of government, debt,
and infringements on our liberties can be reversed.
If that doesn't happen, then a peaceful secession
may become the "least bad" option for many states,
and these states may end up saving the Republic.
If states do secede, I hope it plays out like it does
in this book, without bloodshed or economic collapse.

My story about the future would not be plausible
if I manipulated the past. So, to the best of my
ability, I represented events that happened in or
before 2020 accurately. For example, the Citizenship USA program, Modern Monetary Theory, and
the National Popular Vote Interstate Compact are
real things, even if they are bad ideas. Economic
data was derived from publicly available U.S. government sources or, when not possible, at least

two non-government sources. Historical figures are quoted or summarized faithfully, and the sources of chapter-opening quotes such as Bertolt Brecht and P.J. O'Rourke are quoted with respect. Margaret Thatcher is quoted with reverence. Of course, George Erikson and Jack Moss are completely fictional characters, as are Senators Browning and Gordon, Governor Davis, and President Harris.

People who read my manuscript asked for more data, charts, and examples on a variety of subjects covered in the book. While I am grateful for their interest, I wanted this book to read more like a story than a textbook. Besides, all the interesting data can easily be found elsewhere. My greatest hope is that readers are inspired to learn more about our Constitution, about how far our federal government has drifted from its founding principles, and exactly how much this is costing us.

John Dale
December 2020

ABOUT THE AUTHOR

<u>John Dale</u>

John Dale is a former U.S. military officer and federal employee. He has Bachelor and Master of Arts degrees in the fields of political science, military studies, and economics.

Made in the USA
Middletown, DE
20 September 2021